Out of World

Peter Millett   Joe Sciglitano

NELSON
CENGAGE Learning

Australia • Brazil • Japan • Korea • Mexico • Singapore • Spain • United Kingdom • United States

Out of This World

Text: Peter Millett
Illustrations: Joe Sciglitano
Editor: Vanessa Pellatt
Design: James Lowe
Series design: James Lowe
Production controller: Lisa Porter
Reprint: Siew Han Ong

**Fast Forward Independent Texts
Level 25**

Text © 2009 Cengage Learning Australia Pty Limited
Illustrations © 2009 Cengage Learning Australia Pty Limited

Copyright Notice
This Work is copyright. No part of this Work may be reproduced, stored in a retrieval system, or transmitted in any form or by any means without prior written permission of the Publisher. Except as permitted under the Copyright Act 1968, for example any fair dealing for the purposes of private study, research, criticism or review, subject to certain limitations. These limitations include: Restricting the copying to a maximum of one chapter or 10% of this book, whichever is greater; Providing an appropriate notice and warning with the copies of the Work disseminated; Taking all reasonable steps to limit access to these copies to people authorised to receive these copies; Ensuring you hold the appropriate Licences issued by the Copyright Agency Limited ("CAL"), supply a remuneration notice to CAL and pay any required fees.

ISBN 978 0 17 018001 6
ISBN 978 0 17 017899 0 (set)

Cengage Learning Australia
Level 7, 80 Dorcas Street
South Melbourne, Victoria Australia 3205
Phone: 1300 790 853

Cengage Learning New Zealand
Unit 4B Rosedale Office Park
331 Rosedale Road, Albany, North Shore NZ 0632
Phone: 0508 635 766

For learning solutions, visit **cengage.com.au**

Printed in China by 1010 Printing International Ltd
2 3 4 5 6 7 15

Out of This World

Peter Millett Joe Sciglitano

Contents

Chapter 1	Ice Hockey Fans	4
Chapter 2	The New Goalkeeper	10
Chapter 3	On the Ice	14
Chapter 4	The Invasion	20

Ice Hockey Fans

Sam and Jez were the world's biggest ice hockey fans. It was their favourite sport of all time. They played it everywhere they could, every single day of the year. They played it at school, in the library, in queues at the movies or the bank and even at weddings.

It was the only thing Sam and Jez ever thought about.

Ice Hockey Fans

One day, on their way to a game, they were thinking about ice hockey so much that they didn't even notice a huge glowing object falling from the sky.

CRASH!

It slammed into the ground, sending up a thick cloud of black smoke.

"Jez, how many goals do you think you'll score today?" Sam asked.

"I don't know, four, maybe five …"

Suddenly, a ten-foot-tall alien leapt out from a smoking crater in the ground. It was hairy and massive. It waved its arms in front of Sam and Jez.

The boys halted in their tracks.

Ice Hockey Fans

Sam grabbed Jez's shoulder.
"Hey – wouldn't he make an awesome goalkeeper for our team?"

"Yeah …"

Sam looked up. "Excuse me, have you ever considered playing ice hockey?" he asked.

The alien roared, "Argh! I have come to Earth to learn about your warriors!"

Sam's face lit up. "The Warriors? Why, that's our team – the Northwest Warriors. Come with us and we'll show them to you."

"Earthman, my mission is to find out how strong your warriors are before we invade your planet!" the alien protested.

"Okay. Well, we can talk about that other stuff later if you like, but let's get going now or we'll be late for the game," Jez told him.

The boys rushed off with the alien following closely behind them.

Ice Hockey Fans

The New Goalkeeper

The team was getting ready to go out onto the ice when Sam, Jez and the alien walked up.

Steve was the team captain. "Who's the guy in the fancy dress costume?" he asked.

Jez introduced the alien. "He's our new goalkeeper."

Steve did a double-take. "He's what?"

The New Goalkeeper

Sam walked over to Steve.
"Come on Steve, you've got to let him play for us. He'll be fantastic as our new goalkeeper!"

"But …"

Just then, the referee came up to them.
"We need to start the game right away."

Steve sighed. "Okay! I guess your friend can play for us if he wants to."

Sam handed the alien a goalkeeper's uniform and a hockey stick. "Put this on. It might not fit too well, but it will help to protect your body. Things can get a little dangerous out there on the ice."

Jez looked up at the alien. "I'm sorry, but what did you say your name was?"

"I am Trogg – Warrior Commander from the planet Zartor."

"Oh, hi Trogg. I'm Jez, from Coopers Beach."

The New Goalkeeper

Sam fired a practice shot at Trogg's goal. "Okay Trogg, you have to defend this goal with your life," he said. "Nothing is allowed to get past you. Do you understand? Nothing."

Trogg roared, "I will defend the goal with my life!"

On the Ice

The referee blew her whistle and the game started.

Trogg pulled a small object out of his tool belt and secretly began to scan the players. He recorded how tall and how heavy they were and how fast they moved across the ice. He then pushed a button, sending the information back to the command centre on Zartor.

"Trogg – watch out!" Jez cried.

Suddenly, one of the opponents fired a shot at Trogg's goal. Trogg jumped up and caught the puck between his teeth.

SNAP! He crushed it in two.

"Great save!" Sam said. "But next time, do you mind not eating the sports equipment?"

Halfway through the game, the Northwest Warriors were ahead 10 to zero. Sam and Jez had scored three goals each. Their opponents tried as hard as they could to score, but Trogg's super-fast reactions were too good for them. Trogg used every part of his body to protect the goal – his knees, his nose, the back of his head and all fourteen of his toes.

On the Ice

"Trogg – you're out of this world!" Jez cried, watching him make another incredible save.

When the game ended, the Northwest Warriors had won 25 goals to zero.

"Everyone – three cheers for Trogg!" Sam shouted.

The players lined up and lifted their hockey sticks in the air to give Trogg a hero's send-off. Trogg's smile was almost as wide as the goal.

As Trogg left the ice, his communicator started flashing. It was the command centre on Zartor.

"Trogg, we have processed the information you sent us about Earth's warriors. We know how strong they are and we know how to crush them. Tell us when we should begin the invasion."

Trogg looked over his shoulder to make sure no one was watching. Without saying a word he quietly slipped out of the building.

The Invasion

After the game, Jez and Sam began their long walk home, their minds filled with thoughts about ice hockey. They didn't notice the loud explosion behind them, or the glowing spaceship hurtling up into the sky. They had much more important things to think about – like next week's game.

"So how many goals do you think you'll score next time?" Jez said.

"I don't know, maybe ten, maybe eleven. How about you?"

"Maybe thirteen," Jez replied. "I sure hope that guy Trogg comes back to see us again soon."

"So do I, Jez," Sam said. "And maybe, if we're lucky, next time he might bring some of his friends along!"

Out of This World

Trogg raced across the galaxy to his home planet of Zartor. As he touched down, his commanders rushed out to meet him. Behind them, an army of nearly two million warriors stood, ready to begin the invasion.

The Invasion

Trogg sprinted towards them.
"Stop! Stop!" he cried. "We must stop the invasion of Earth immediately!"

A loud roar of protest went up.

"I have found something much better for our warriors to do instead of making war …"

Out of This World

Trogg held his hockey stick high above his head.
"It is called ice hockey!"